To Grandma Barbara for introducing me to Harpo and Chico,
and to Harpo and Chico for being Harpo and Chico
—E.K.

For my funny and unforgettable teachers,
Marian Edson and Nancy Krim
—A.T.

Balzer + Bray is an imprint of HarperCollins Publishers.

Sharko and Hippo
Text copyright © 2020 by Elliott Kalan
Illustrations copyright © 2020 by Andrea Tsurumi
All rights reserved. Manufactured in Italy.

ISBN 978-0-06-279109-2

The artist used Sumi ink, nibs, watercolor, collage, and Photoshop to create the illustrations for this book.
Typography by Dana Fritts
20 21 22 23 24 RTLO 10 9 8 7 6 5 4 3 2 1
❖
First Edition

SHARKO AND HIPPO

By

Elliott Kalan

Illustrated by

Andrea Tsurumi

BALZER + BRAY
An Imprint of HarperCollinsPublishers

My name's Sharko,
because I'm a shark.

And Hippo's
called Hippo, because
Hippo is a hippo.

Forget the pole!

I can't use the pole unless I have the bait.

So, give me the bait.

I apologize. I shouldn't lose my temper.

Hippo, the bait is in a can.

Give me the can.

That's not a can! That's a cone.

Why do you give me all these crazy things, Hippo?! What kind of friend are you? You never give me the thing I need!